THE BIG LITTLE BANG

Randy Dingwall

Merry Christmas Berad

For Your Bro

Randy D

TABLE OF CONTENTS

YO

Hello, I am Galaglaw, from the Sesqua clan. The Sesqua along with the Nogad have been trying to correct the transgressions of the one we called Tar, since the days of the Big Little Bang. Our adventure covers an interval spanning over fourteen million years. It is a long and complex tale. There are few Sesqua left on earth and the numbers of the Nogad, are even lower. I fear if I do not share this story that you may never hear it.

We came to this planet when it was a young world. Our goal had never been to conquer. What brought us here was the sheer will to survive. Leaving our home planet was not our choice. My ancestors set their sights on the only sanctuary they could see, the planet Earth.

***

When the last of the large pig like creatures called entelodonts wandered the plains and bushland of earth that is when my ancestors first entered earth's atmosphere. One thousand ships flew as if they were one The Nogad at the controls making subtle adjustments, turning with the ease and absent-minded precision of a flock of birds. They cruised over vast grasslands and forests of dragon blood trees. The crafts banked towards the ocean, skirting past young mountains not yet weathered by wind and rain.

The Nogad marveled at the beauty and diversity of this young planet. Eagles and hawks circled as they rode thermal currents high into the sky, watching for small rodents scurrying among the tall grasses of the savannah. My ancestors glimpsed a large herd of mastodons, just before the beasts vanished under the forests protective canopy. Scores of apes and chimpanzees were evolving, along with many herbivores. Creating the predators that feasted on them. Predators like the saber tooth tigers, and their ocular cousins the false saber tooth cats.

Otter frolicked in the kelp beds that ringed the coastlines, slipping into the oceans depths. The Nogad found a less crowded ocean then exists today. There were fish, baleen whales, and several varieties of shark, including the Megalodon shark.

As I have mentioned I am Galaglaw, you may call me Glaw. The Nogad are pale skinned, rather non-descript beings, when at rest. Motion changes that, sending ripples of energy through their systems. The vivid colors pulsating inside and around the craft are spectacular to witness.

The Nogad craft described by humans as looking like flying saucers or discs. From your perspective that is understandable. In fact, and purely coincidentally, the ships look more like a large clam, rather than a dinner plate. These creatures fascinate the Nogad, you would think they were related the way they carry on about them.

The Nogad are the creators and the pilots of their crafts. Masters of organic technologies, they live their long lives inside their ships and inside their minds. They are the keepers of our history, and the ones that can see. Even to the Sesqua, who are family, the Nogad ways are a mystery we do not fully understand.

The Sesqua are the hunters and gatherers of the society and we would have it no other way. The explorers of land and sea we are robust creatures. Standing over seven feet tall, we enjoy our physical prowess. Full of life, we are sometimes impulsive and often mischievous as is the nature of youth. We still take our role seriously. It is the Sesqua, who must gather the materials needed by the Nogad to advance our future technologies.

The Nogad whom we respectfully call our elders had foresaw the doom of our planet, and developed the propulsion system needed to get us here. Life on earth when my ancestors first got here was exciting. This was a completely new world to explore. They did have to keep their wits about them as many large predators roamed the lands and swam in the oceans. Overall, the Nogad and Sesqua had few concerns and for millions of years, they roamed freely.

The Sesqua explored the land during the cool nights, returning to the ocean during the heat of the day. Well the Nogad flew their ships day and night, not worried about the curious eyes below, trying to perfect the propulsion system that had managed to get us to earth, but was not yet powerful enough to allow us to leave.

We watched as over one hundred species of apes evolved, witnessed the cloven-footed mammals as they diversified and became a multitude of species. We intervened as little as possible, since our plan was to leave this planet when we could break free of its atmosphere. We would have left sooner if it had not been for one fateful event involving two young Sesqua, Tar and Eris called the Big Little Bang.

**

BIG LITTLE BANG

On a deserted beach the wind wails a mournful tale. A wet hand covered in fur reaches out of the ocean's black depths and comes to rest on a partially submerged rock. Water beads silently rolling off its fingertips, the hairs on the fingers dry. Appearing to stand on end as if listening. The oceans waves tamed by the shelter of the bay slap the coastline with little conviction. Their energy spent, they retreat.

Tar's head slowly rises from the black depths. His eyes as dark as his name, reflect no light as they quickly scan the rocky beach. He sniffs the salty air, senses fully aware. Taking a moment to adjust to the change in environment he listens to the wind howl through the tree tops. Then silently rising from the water, disturbing nary a ripple, he dashes across the rocky beach. Picking his way each footstep carefully placed.

He has arrived on this beach on the darkest of nights. His senses on high alert, he quickly finds the concealment of the forest. Covered in a dense fur and a layer of blubber he is a thick bodied muscular specimen. Standing over seven feet tall on two massive tree stumps, masquerading as legs. He is quick, light and agile on his feet.

Tar pauses as the wind screams through the trees, his sensitive ears picking up the smallest vibrations on the air. A faint sound he feels more than hears comes from his left. Hairs on his neck bristling. Every muscle in his body now coiled ready to spring, his attention focused on his quarry. He stalks silently but quickly, a hundred yards turns into a mere fifteen feet, Tar pounces covering the final distance in a single bound.

A growl escapes his throat, Tars prey having already sensed his presence is incredibly agile. Ducking at the last moment it avoids the full impact of the attack. The glancing blow sending them both rolling down the hill. They tumbled over a small cliff, landing together in a heap of leaves on the forest floor. A shriek of joy escapes Tars lips, the sound echoing across the bay.

He is like a little kid, not much thought and a lot of action, he loved to sneak up on Eris. It is a playful game, but also a useful skill in this new world.These young Sesqua consider the ocean their home, venturing onto land only for short periods of time to gather the materials and supplies not readily available to them in the ocean.

Eris enjoys Tars playful nature and allows him to think he snuck up on her. She is more reserved then Tar but towers over him in stature, even with a slightly stooped posture. The large female's fur is lighter than her mates jet-black coat. Normally a gentle thoughtful creature, she is not feeling right on this night.

It was Tar's impulsive nature and natural curiosity about all life forms, which has led them to observe the creatures developing in this area. This was their favorite place to explore. They had been coming to this area for years to forage for some of the strange items the Nogad request.

Tar and Eris enjoyed looking for materials, it was like a game and they always found a way to enjoy their chores. Back then, the Nogad wanted them to collect as much monazite sand and iron containing cobalt as they could. Eris was ready for a night of hunting treasures. Tar had his mind on other matters, he had taken a special interest in this region but they were not the same reasons Eris had.

Tar is fascinated in the creatures that he and Eris have been observing. She does not share her mate's interest in them. This had become a regular occurrence lately when they come to this area, so she decides to wander off to sniff out the cobalt on her own.

Leaving Tar alone, settling in to watch the creatures. They are half his height and smaller boned. The small group of apes are returning home after a day of foraging for insects, grains and small animals. They were hunters and gatherers. This maybe what fueled Tar's interest, he knew he was there to observe not interact. He had been watching this group for some time now, curious about their personal interactions and choices in food.

Only staying in an area until the supplies dwindled or competition drove them away, they lived a nomadic life. This area was a good area and they had not moved for several years. Their nesting area this night was in a small patch of fruit trees that bordered a large river.

Along the river edge, the small apes have dug holes in the ground allowing the water to seep into these basins. Giving them safe cleaner drinking water in an area away from the crocodiles patrolling the murky water.

It is in one particular drinking hole located under a large fruit tree that Tar has noticed with great curiosity, the changes in personal interaction and movement of the creatures after they had consumed from the one particular basin. The sweet pungent odor drifting in the wind finds his flared nostrils perking his interest.

Tar waits until there is no movement in the small clearing below, the creatures having fallen asleep high in the treetops. Confident in his stalking talent, Tar cautiously approaches the strange smelling liquid, which has caught his interest. He takes a sip and then another, the alcohol levels in the crude mead are minimal.

The effects on a body that had never consumed alcohol before are immediate. Attempting to return to the beach after his consumption of the fermented fruit does not succeed. Tar makes it a few hundred yards before he falls, laying sprawled out in a daze near the apes nesting area.

High in the branches one set of eyes peeking between the leaves has been watching this whole scene. When he had first approached her body tensed, a scream of alarm catching in her throat, she fell silent not wanting to bring attention to her group hidden in the trees. She watched as he entered the clearing, she had noticed this creature in the distance on other nights. An instinct told her, he meant them no harm. Now with the creature sprawled a mere hundred yards away, she cautiously climbs down from her hiding spot hugging the ground as she approaches.

The female's curiosity brings her closer, she is in heat and the scent that she inhales stimulates her desires even more. She grunts at the creature that lays sprawled on its back before her. There is no response. She looks around nervously sensing no eyes on them, she moves closer. Her breath warming the object of her primitive curiosity, it stirs, growing larger as she watches fascinated her eyes transfixed her breathing deepens.

He awakens, startled confused but fully aroused, looking up their eyes meet as she reaches out to hold his swollen member in her hand. Tar, still in an alcohol-induced daze instantly responds. Letting out a deep grunt, he stands to tower over her, she turns raising her butt to meet him as he mounts her. His thrusts unrestrained, yet silent, the mating ends quickly. The young ape does not glance back as she returns to her perch.

Tar wanders back towards the beach not at his regular pace. The closer he gets to his destination the worse he feels. His memory usually crystal clear is having problems organizing the night activities.

Waiting for him, Eris is swimming just off shore. Having spent the night collecting materials she is exhausted and she finds the water relaxing. She has a story of her own to share but she listens first as Tar recounts his fuzzy thoughts.

Sniffing the foul odor on his breath, the memories Tar shares of his adventures brings a great sadness to Eris. She realizes he is not himself. This strange liquid has changed his logic. Listening to his thoughts a dark cloud slips unnoticed into her mind, infiltrating her thoughts.

She falls silent, deciding to share her news another day. The two young Sequa swim out of the bay in silence, none of their usual playfulness in evidence. Eris continues to mull over the event as they dive down to a depth of two hundred fathoms where their Nogad ship has been waiting patiently.

***

LOST TRIBE

The Nogad houses all heard about Tar's one night tryst. Deciding what to do was not easy, the discussion went on for many years. Eris argued vehemently over this time her irritation evident. She wanted the breeds eradicated believing the best time was when their numbers were low. Arguing with the Nogad got her nowhere.

Her relationship with Tar had only become more distant. His stubborn refusal to apologize for his actions angered her even more. Her rage replaced by shock when the Nogad of Tar's house made their final decision, one that all the Nogad houses agreed with.

The actions of Tar were hard to understand even for the wise Elders. The Nogad and Sesqua did not use mind-altering drugs they had no need. Therefore, it took many movements before they understand his actions understanding did not mean forgiveness. Once they decided there was no mercy shown, for some actions the Nogad believe, you only get one chance.

They declared that, "anyone who has sex with an animal must be put to death." The Nogad could not believe they had to make that rule. Tar died a quick and painless death. It was the only compassion shown by the Nogad that day. Eris and her children mourned alone.

As far as the developing species were concerned, the Nogad decided to take a wait and see attitude. Tar's transcending, transgressions were not the apes fault.

Eris's mind raced after Tars death, she had always been one to overthink situations, she mulled over what the Nogad had decided. She twisted it this way and that repeatedly in her mind, rethinking it a thousand times and then a million more. Eventually, the edges became blurred, a whirlpool of thoughts and possibilities being sucked into a central focus point. No matter where they begin, they all end with the same conclusion. Logic loses its grasp flooding her being, not allowing her any rest. Deteriorating, mental and physical thoughts mutated, she slips into a sullen dark mood that she could not shake. One that Eris would never lose.

Eris had always respected her elders, that respect was gone. She hated Tar for what he had done. He had still been the father of her son Dys and daughter Hys, who would now grow up without his guidance. She became bitter more withdrawn, eventually deciding to take her two young children with her. She left her Nogad home behind never looking back.

They slipped away on a star filled night, abandoning their elders, living out their remaining years in the wild. For thousands of years they wandered the earth. The Nogad do not know the history of Eris's clan, they never returned for their final visit. The history we have are rumours from humans, and information gathered by the Sesqua scouts.

Eris had isolated herself and her children from all others and she now had time to launch the idea that had been growing inside her mind like a cancer, eating the core of what was once a gentle soul. She always wanted to act on her beliefs. She wanted the developing humanoids eliminated, that is all she cared about now.

Fueled by a frustration and a rage she did not understand, she set off to find her prey. The Nogad decision had taken centuries, the humanoids had spread out across the land in small groups. Some individuals hidden in larger populations were hard to find, Eris may have well succeeded in her goal if not for the illogical hatred she felt for the breeds. That made her do irrational things.

On one of her first hunts, she found a family group relaxing by a small meadow. The gentle Sesqua, now turned into a cold-blooded killer, vented all her rage. Eris ripped the limbs from their bodies, stomping on them in an attempt to return them to the earth, the children besides her jumping up and down, their excited calls egging Eris on. Their eyes wide and wild, Dys and Hys are ecstatic, running about slapping the trees and pounding the ground, applauding the carnage.

Eris, spurred on and not yet satisfied, stomps around the clearing her eyes land on body of one of the dead. She grabs the skull of the lifeless corpse, ripping it from its torso. Her large thumbs snuggly fit into the eye sockets, with little effort she splits the skull in two, feasting on the brains that spill onto the ground. As if trying to take back the gift her unfaithful mate had given them. An impulsive, repulsive act, she could not have known the affects her new diet would have on the three of them.

Eris may have been more successful on her mission if it had not been for the effects eating brains had on her mind and that of her children. Already suffering unbalanced thoughts, now a disease inflicted them. Its effects shortening their lives and clouding their thoughts even more. The symptoms not as harmful as they would be to humans still did not help Dys and Hys's social development.

Dys and Hys guided only by the tortured memories of their mother, having never known an elder's wise intervention, grew up wild, irresponsible, lawless creatures. Eris traveled the world with her children for almost two thousand years. Their time together filled with chaos, conflict and infighting, they were not a happy family.

Eris her mind addled bore many children with Dys over the years, the despicable acts not given a second thought by her lawless son. One of these creations was a creature named Pho. This spawn was born with a murderess nature. Pho at a tender age slaughtered his mother Eris, while she slept, in many ways it was a merciful death. When you consider the atrocities, she had committed in her lifetime.

The legends of the Eris's offspring are worldwide. It is proof that what happened the night of the Big Little Bangs affected not only the evolution of the human race. Many have suffered on both sides.

Eris's children were not been given a fair chance, raised by a mother full of strife. Left to find their own paths with no guidance, Dys and Hys had often interbred, or had sex with lower forms of animals. The resulting species had shorter lives than their parents had and developed many different body shapes and traits, some becoming bound to the land. The children knew that mating with animals ended any possibilities of them ever rejoining the Nogad. Dys and Hys were past caring, there was no going back for them.

No life form can evolve with only two parents. Hys and Dys realized this was impossible. Trying to track the genetic history of Eris's clan is not possible, it is a big world and we have traveled a long ways through earth's time.

Many of the creatures that evolved from Eris's kin, died out in the great extinction event 70,000 years ago, a few survived down through the centuries. Taking many paths, not all of them bad, they go by a variety of names the world over. Their stories becoming folklore and legend. I should mention a few that I am sure are Eris's kin.

After Eris's death, her children had not stayed together for very long. Dys the male had wandered off one day and Hys had not followed him. Dys went west, his descendants eventually ending up in the areas now known as North and South America.

Hys had remained closer to her roots, her kin seeping out of the region in a circular pattern eventually reaching as far south as Australia.

Bigfoot or Sasquatch are two names recognized by people as the most famous of these creatures. To save confusion one should understand a few important facts.

Sesqua when on scouting missions may be mistaken for Sasquatches. The easiest way to explain this is Sesqua are always Sasquatches to human eyes. What humans call Sasquatches are not always Sesquas.

We are not loud tree throwing chest-thumping creatures. The Sesqua are usually quiet, going about our chores and rarely having any contact with humans, except occasional fleeting encounters.

Some humans can see us but this is rare. We consider these people gifted, a gift we do not fully understand. Fortunately, the gifted ones are not the ones that would try to kill us. We can pick up the energy of a killer from miles away so they are easy to avoid.

There are a few of Eris's descendants who have killed humans for sport over the centuries, some of her kin have been a real pain in the ass, not all of them, just a few.

North American Native legend, usually describes the Sasquatch as tall, between six and ten feet in height with a body weighing over five hundred pounds, covered in a dense dark brownish red fur. Apparently, a foul odor follows the beasts around which people can smell from over one hundred yards away. Personally, I find this a little offensive. Humans really do not smell that great, but we do not make a big deal about it. Sometimes if you do not have anything good to say, you should be quiet, that is my opinion, I know I should not take it personally. The truth is we have an earthy natural musk. That smells like a mix of pine needles and steamed seaweed, wrapped in a mossy coat of fresh fish heads.

Several of the creatures known as Sasquatch are gentle benevolent souls who would never hurt a human. The Natives of Bella Coola also had some of Dys descendants living in their woods. They named him Boqs and recognized him as a malevolent evil, dangerous creature, who given a chance would eat humans and rape their woman.

They describe the Boqs as having facial features of a human, walking upright with a slightly stooped posture. Their arms extending past the knees as did another appendage. There are many stories about the well-endowed Boqs.

Spending as much time on land as in the ocean, Boqs were not the malevolent creatures the Bella Coola believed them to be. Sure, they made a lot of noise if they were frightened and tried to bluff their way out of situations. However, they never killed humans. Sometimes when we do not understand something we think the worse, everyone does it.

***

Qaklas a brave from Bella Coola was camped with his wife and child in the Bay of a Thousand Islands, when all three of them heard a loud commotion in the bushes behind their camp. Picking up his rifle, Qaklas yelled into the night, "GO AWAY" the commotion only seemed to grow louder.

Frightened for his wife and child brave yelled again, "GET OUT OF HERE, OR YOU WILL FEEL MY POWER," the sounds grew louder. He punctuated his warnings with a few rounds of ammunition, sent in the general direction of the noise. The gunshots unleashed an orchestra of screams and grunts accompanied by the pounding and breaking of branches.

Now truly concerned for his family's safety, he hurried them into the canoe and guarded their passage with his rifle as they paddled out into the shallows. There they anchored and waited for Qaklas to join them. As the family huddled in the canoe, they could hear the Bogs on the shoreline making a tremendous racket. There was no way they could have understood, that the creatures were trying to warn them.

Sitting in their canoe in the middle of the bay the family noticed how quiet it had become. There was no wind not a ripple disturbed the water's surface, not a sound could be heard and it had a peaceful yet eerie feeling.

Then as if out of nowhere, the canoe began to pitch back and forth, as if in heavy seas. Qaklas picked up his oar and began to paddle as fast as he could. Planning to make his escape to Resolution Bay, he had made it only a short distance when his paddle struck bottom.

His mind raced, "How could this be?" he wondered.

They were still in the middle of the channel when he

jumped out of the canoe. Realizing the water was only up

to his knees, he dragged the canoe with his wife and child

through the mud, as he trudged along the shoreline all the

way to Resolution Bay.

With the Boqs following along behind their

celebration misunderstood, Boqs were simple creatures.

They had realized there was an earthquake and possible

landslides. They had tried their best to warn the young

family.

The natives of Bella Coola were a wise and

observant people. However, even they could misjudge if

not given all the facts. In the game of life, sometimes safe

is better than sorry. Later in this book, I have shared the

story of Sente. He was a man who visited the nearby village

of Bella Bella many years ago. Well there he had a

conversation with a member of that tribe named Brave.

***

Living a short distance from Bella Coola on the rock now called Vancouver Island. The coastal natives had dealings with many of the Dys kin. They recorded these encounters in their many stories. The Basket Ogress is one of his children they met and here is one of those stories. Basket Ogress or Tsonqua, two of her many names, was a soul wasted away by hate and desperation. One who would steal children, carrying them home in her cedar basket were she would feast on them. At least that is how most tell the story.

This legend is about one of the last in a tortured line of Dys kin, a creature driven mad by isolation and loneliness. Her body frail and about to die, fleeting moments of sanity, only magnify her pain. She has terrorized the natives in this area for centuries. Her need for company driving her to do unspeakable acts, she has abducted many children over the years in an attempt to quench her loneliness.

Not a capable mother her attempts at raising them failed, unfortunately when they died she was not squeamish about eating the remains. Horrifying as this was to the natives, it was an instinctive survival strategy as far as her addled mind was concerned.

One night Basket Ogress was sneaking around a native village. A young girl thinking she heard sounds, is in her bed crying. Her grandmother tries to frighten the child.

Saying to her, "Go to sleep, else the Basket Ogress will come and carry you away!"

The little girl shivers in her bed but wanting to overcome her fears, goes outside for a quick look. Quickly returning to her home were her grandmother asks her.

"Why are you afraid? It is just a big person with hairy hands" she teases, "They are only trying to frighten you, go back outside."

The little girl wanting to show her grandmother she was not afraid and that she was brave, turns and walks outside. The parents and grandmother heard a blood-curdling scream! Basket Ogress picks the young girl up in her arms and whisks her off to an underground lair she used when in the area.

The parents in hot pursuit follow her and can hear the cries of their child underneath the earth. Grabbing tools they tried to dig her out, sometimes the cries were near, then would fade as Basket Ogress moved farther into the labyrinth of tunnels she had dug.

After many hours of digging, heartbroken and grief stricken, they return to their village. When the coast was clear, Ogress took the young child on a journey to her home. The child still with her wits about her left a trail of broken hemlock branches. Hoping that her parents might follow or she could escape and find her own way home.

Arriving at her dwelling the lonely Basket Ogress tries to make the child comfortable. Offering her some dried meat and tallow to eat with crab apples and dried berries for dessert. The shelters walls covered in animal skins protect a small fire in the corner which throws ghostly shadows across the dirt floor. Basket Ogress has been watching the natives for years, learning their language and ways. The young native girl who does not seem to fear her, fascinates basket Ogress, she notices the ear ornaments in the child's ears.

Ogress asks, "Oh, oh, how was it done, your ear ornaments are nice, can I wear them?"

"Do you have holes in your ears?" asked the girl.

"I have no holes in my ears, but you can make holes in my ears."

"No, you would not be able to handle the pain that I endured when my father punched holes in my ears," replied the girl.

The Basket Ogress believes she can handle the pain, "How were the holes driven?" she asks.

"With branches like these," said the girl, picking up a handful of branches she tells Basket Ogress, "Lay on your back, and tell me where your hammer is so I might drive them through?"

She then took a branch striking it with all her might, the ogress screamed in pain, begging the young girl to stop.

"Don't do this, don't do this," she cried.

Her words are in vain. The child strikes again, the branch going right through the ear, penetrating the brain.

The creature utters a final, "Oh!" before she dies, lying lifeless on the dirt floor.

Not yet sure the creature is dead, the girl drives another branch through the opposite ear, now certain she is dead the child pushed her into the fire and burns her.

Returning home, she follows the trail of broken branches she has left, arriving at the village where her own burial is taking place. She hears the mourning song sung in her honor. Her appearance shocks the village. They stand and stare, her parents faint from the shock. Finally, one brave arose picking up the child.

He asks, "What was it that took you?"

"It was the Basket Ogress that carried me away."

"How did you save yourself?"

"She wanted my ear ornaments," I said, "you could not endure the pain, I endured at my father's hand that is how I did it, I punched holes through the ears of Basket Ogress and now she is dead."

The tribe follows the trail back to the dwelling. The natives returned to their village with baskets of cranberries, dried fruit, meat, berries and many animal skins. The girl's father has a big party, giving away all the animal skins his generosity earning him status as a Chief.

The Nogad or Sesqua held no party, Basket Ogress had been a lost tortured soul and she had wanted to connect with humans. Whatever you say about her, I believe she was misunderstood. I recovered her ashes and returned them to the sea.

We return all Sequa that die on land back to their Nogad house, we try to show the same respect for all of Eris's clan, but we have not found them all. If we cannot find them, the chances of you discovering them are close to zero.

***

The story of the Basket Ogress, reminds me of the story told by the clan of the Nimpkish in Northern B.C. called, "The Boy who went underground" although I cannot be sure, it sounds like the Basket Ogress spent time in the North, as the story goes.

A boy, who was of noble blood from the family of the Famous-ones, was hungry and crying. His parents tried to quiet him but were unable to silence the child. Eventually the parents fell asleep. The boy continued to cry, he cried so hard that his eyes began to swell.

Then someone from the other side of the big house yelled, "Try to quiet your son," but the boy's parents heard nothing and remained asleep.

Suddenly the ground opened and the boy disappeared. His cries heard under the earth, sometimes on one corner of the house, then moving to another. The parents finally awoke from their slumber.

Everyone asked them, "Do you know where your son is?"

The parent called to their son and could hear his answering cries, they picked up shovels and tried to dig were they heard his voice, but they could not find him and eventually gave up.

Having never met the Basket Ogress, they had no way of making sense of the disappearance. The only evidence they found was a belly of a rotten salmon a dog had dragged into the big house, they assumed the boy must have eaten it, and gone mad. That was why he had disappeared. Well the Basket Ogress terrorized natives in North America. The Mapinguari was raising a little hell of its own in South America.

***

In the Brazilian jungles lived the foul Mapinguari, also known as Ishashi. They always stayed close to water, I have hunted many of these creatures over the years. Last time I was in Brazil, the only Mapinguari in existence had gone completely mad over some cows. The mad Map had killed no humans, but I would rather be safe than sorry.

For three weeks, spanning March and April of that year, the last of the Mapinguari went on a rampage terrorizing the small farming community of Barra das Garas, which is located a full ten days hike from the city people call Cuiab.

Reports in all the major newspapers of Rio de Janeiro and San Paulo said over one hundred cattle had been slaughtered by someone or something with super human strength. Many of the cows had no tongues. It appeared they had been ripped out, when the cattle were still standing. Locals reported seeing Map many times but he proved to be very elusive. The tracks in the area were eighteen inches long and were humanoid like in shape.

Picking up Maps trail was not a problem, this creature stunk, yeah I admit it this animal smelt bad. I do not wish to share the details of this hunt having hunted the lost souls of Dys descendants for longer then I care to remember there is no joy in this chore. The innocence of Sesqua youth has never been the same since the days of Tar. The stigma of his actions have stayed with the houses that bore Tar and Eris.

There was another animal living in the jungles of South America, the Maroxi are a race of humanoids. There have been many sightings in the South American jungles a man named Perry Fawcett met a group of them in the early 1900s, he said they lived in villages and hunted with bows and arrows. The shy bush people were afraid of humans, but chose the fight instead of flight tactic, which ended up being their demise. Humans have a history of eliminating their completion, or anything they do not understand.

***

Eris's offshoots did not only end up in North and South America. In China, the province of Tibet was home to the Yeti, often mistaken for the Meh Teh Lama. The Yeti is a result of the coevolution of Hys and an old world monkey, who settled in the Himalayas. The animals enjoyed the cold climate, growing long white hair that blended into the snow. They were reclusive beings living in small bands or alone. Modern day reports on the Yeti date back to the early years often described as mean spirited, man like creatures, likely to kill humans and eat them given half a chance. Incredibly strong, very few people have ever seen the Yeti the most compelling evidence being their footprints.

Not all accounts of the Yeti describe them as creatures to be feared. Captain d'Auvergne who was from Calcutta claimed that he had become lost while on a hike in the Himalaya Mountains. Alone, injured, he was beginning to lose hope, blinded by the snow he was in danger of dying from exposure, when a Yeti found him and showed him kindness.

He reported that a pre-historic human had picked him up and carried him several miles to the shelter of a cave. Where it kept him warm and fed him until he was able to return home on his own. Four years later Slavomir Rawicz, the author of the bestselling book, "The Long Walk." In the book, he tells the story of escaping from a Siberian war camp. In addition, how he and his companions made their way to India by crossing the Himalayas.

In his account of the journey, he describes how he and six friends came across two eight-foot tall creatures playing in the snow. The location of the encounter said to have been between Bhutan and Sikkam, Rawicz and his men watched the creatures from a distance of one hundred yards for over two hours with no incidences.

The individuality of Eris's kin is undeniable. The paths they took were often difficult, I can understand their love of the climate, but it was too far from their original ocean home. The last time we recovered remains of a Yeti from the Himalayas, was in the year 2000.

One cannot mention the Yeti without talking about the most famous of China's creatures. Sometimes a memory lives deep inside the subconscious passed down from generation to generation, never rising to the surface. The descendants of the original thought never fulling understanding their own customs and beliefs. A child slips the last of their dinner under the bed to appease the boogeyman, a father leaves a shot of liquor on the porch for his ancestors at least that is the reason they think they did it the real reason lost in time.

***

Humanoids evolving around the South China Sea, one hundred and fifty thousand years ago, all had dealings with the giant ape Gigantopithecus blacki, the name they go by today. They were gigantic animals as the names implies reaching ten feet in height and weighing over one thousand pounds, blacki was an intimidating beast, powerful jaws held huge molars and massive canines, often ground down by the grit and dirt they consumed well foraging.

The humanoids in this area realized the creature that could snap a tiger's back with one blow, was a docile creature that did not look at them as a meal. Gigantopithecus would only become violent if attacked or it felt the need to protect their young, spending the majority of their days swimming and lounging in the water.

The gentle giants grazed on several varieties of aquatic plants, only venturing onto land in the cool of the night to munch on bamboo and other grasses. Being out of the water for long periods could be stressful for a bi pedal creature, weighing over half a ton. For years, they lived beside the humanoids and no conflict ever arose.

One day one of Hys descendants wandered into the region that is now China, over ten feet tall, she rarely came across creatures that could match her in size and strength. Therefore, you can imagine her surprise and excitement when she came across this race of giant apes.

To make a long story short, the alpha male of the group mated with the female spawning a creature that would grow over eighteen feet tall, inheriting all the evil nature and spite of his grandmother Eris. Seldom did the gentle nature of his Gigantopithecus father rise to the surface.

He was born sterile, which is often the fate of such abominations. His impotence did nothing to improve his disposition. He grew up quickly, his strength soon unmatched even by his mother, his evil nature reasoning that if he could not sire offspring none should. He killed all the young and then hunted down every male in a thousand mile radius, ripping them asunder and spreading their bones to warn all others. He ruled his domain with no challengers.

The locals told stories of this creature, standing taller than the combined height of three men. The echoes of his calls and chest thumping invaded their dreams, his bloody exploits and love for human flesh became a constant worry.

The natives moved into the thickest area of the forest where the king did not enter. The first human sacrifices happened in this area, in hopes of appeasing the creature. The frightened villagers left their dead at the forest edge so the beast would not be tempted to enter. The memories of these events hide in the subconscious of your ancestors.

The king of the Gigantopithecus lived for a short time. Yet his memory has risen to inspire stories like "King Kong" and the gentler kid friendly "Jungle Book." As far as names go, you have to admit King Kong has a certain regal tone to it.

Just a little west of China in an area now called

Russia lived the Almos. The need to survive can take any

animal on a wild ride, Eris's kin had almost all died off.

The insanity passed down did not help in most of their

attempts, nature is resourceful, not all her children inherited

her hatred for the humans or her destructive nature.

Some developed a respect and admiration for

humans and tried with the help of ocular evolution, to join

the human race. If you have been paying attention you have

noticed the word "ocular" used a couple of times, I have

explained the process of ocular and tactile evolution in the

final chapter.

Many failed, but one of the most successful

attempts was by a Hys descendent, by the name of Zana.

This woman off the woods did not have many years left on

this earth and she was old and feeble for an Almas. Zana

was a wild woman, no doubt about that, but she did have

her softer side. The Almos live in the mountains near

T'khina, less than a two-mile hike from Sukhumi
Abkhazia, in the Caucasus Mountains.

Almost one hundred years ago, some locals
captured Zana, she did not appreciate being kidnapped
fighting violently with them. She soon calmed down and fit
into the community, doing odd chores and eventually
hooking up with a man named Edgi Genaba, whom she had
several children with, it was said the children looked
human but most died at birth. The people blamed Zana's
genetic differences for the deaths. Soon after, she gave
birth to two healthy boys, Dzhanda and Khwit and two
girls, named Kodzhanar and Gamasa,

Zana died an old and satisfied human. They tested
her son's skull when he died. People were convinced they
would find Neanderthal DNA or maybe something even
stranger. He passed all tests and was classified a human, his
bloodline absorbed into the human race.

Her clan the Almas had inhabited the Caucasus and Pamir mountains for centuries, described by the locals as "more like wild people then ape." They stood on two legs, standing between five feet and six and a half feet tall, with flat noses and a prominent brow ridge. The Almas some have compared to Neanderthal man in appearance.

The local indigenous people have stories going back hundreds of years concerning their interactions with the Almos, who often communicated with them using hand gestures when bartering for food and trinkets. The Almas children played with the human children and neither had fear, so the story goes. I am happy Zana found peace here on this earth, not many of Eris's descendants have found peace.

The natives, who knew the Almos, also knew of a hominoid named Chucunaa or Chuchunya, who were not as friendly as the Almos. According to the locals, they would sometimes attack killing humans and eating their flesh. I think they were the last in a line of the Neanderthals. Their extinction was not an easy one. The proud species driven by starvation resorted to cannibalism and acts of pure barbarisms in the end.

Neanderthals, with no interference, could have evolved into the smartest most dominant animals on earth, if it had not been for the evolutionary head start Tar had given to humans. Stocky, stronger, smarter the gentler Neanderthals would have been a worthy steward of earth, if the humans has not seen the need to eliminate any competition they found.

Although not all Neanderthals died off, some managed to interbreed with humans around forty thousand years ago and were absorbed into the human race. There are rumors among the Sesqua that the Neanderthals had mated with Tar's descendants, possibly as far back as six hundred thousand years ago, but there is no way of confirming this.

The Neanderthals were stocky strong creatures, seldom reaching a height over six feet they loved to hunt at night having excellent night vision. However, found direct sunlight hard on their eyes, their large brains understood the need for balance. Humans seem incapable of grasping this concept. It is true they had light colored skin, although it concealed under a thick coat of dark brown, reddish hair. Some wore the most basic clothing, but most roamed naked and never lost their lustrous coats until the end when mange took them.

***

In India one of Hys descendants mated with a species of old world monkeys. That evolved into the Colobinae group, which includes over fifty species and ten genera. Out of this stew of creativity emerged the Mande Burung, who now lives in the northeastern state of Meghalaya, India. The mountains in this area are the Garo Hills, with peaks rising 1400 metres above sea level. This area well known for having some of the densest forest and jungle in all of India, charting this vast area is nearly impossible. Many areas have never felt the footsteps of man or Sesqua.

The abundance of natural medicine and edible vegetation made it the perfect location for the shy reclusive Mande, who is a devout vegetarian. The description given by the few that have seen them might lead you to believe they were describing a Sasquatch or Yeti. Unfortunately, the animal known as Mande Burung is almost extinct. Their limited numbers combined with their reclusive nature have not helped their cause and there have even been reports of deformed Burung spotted. I can only hope that those reports are not true, they were such a peaceful beast never harming human or other animals. Nearby in Indonesia was another fascinating animal.

Little Bigfoot, is one of the most interesting animals around, going by the names Sarajung gigi or Orang Penduk which when translated from Indonesian means, "Short person." Living mainly on a diet of fruits and vegetables, it is an opportunist. Eating a varied diet, enjoying ginger root, fruits, vegetables, insects, crabs and anything else they can scavenge.

Debbie Martyr, a prominent researcher with decades of research on the Orang Penduk has interviewed thousands of witnesses over the years and has seen the animal herself many times. Describing it as no more than 85 to 90 cm tall, that is less than 3 feet for those metrically challenged. Although she said, she had seen a few that were a little larger.

Their hair was either grey or black. Debbie goes on to describe them as having a prominent brow ridge above the eyes with a sweeping forehead reminiscent of a gorilla. The face distinctly humanoid, the "Short person" when frightened is said to bare its teeth showing off its large canines, this is a purely defensive warning.

The villagers of Kininci have great respect for the "Short persons" power. They have tremendous upper body strength, with strong arms and a massive barrel chest able to uproot trees and snap the vines of the rattan as if they were matchsticks. For all their strength, they have skinny little legs and tiny rather delicate feet.

I do not have to explain to you what the Orang Penduk is or were they came from. The explanations given by the local people and the experts that have studied these animals saves me the effort. The first theory is that it is a case of mistaken identity. People are just getting confused and misidentifying local animals.

The second theory is that people are seeing a previously unidentified species of primate. The third and final possibility is much like the second theory. People suggest that it may be a previously undocumented species of early hominoid, still living in the Samarian jungle. I will let you draw your own conclusions on the Little Bigfoot

named Sarajung gigi.

***

Eris's offspring did not evolve into Almos,

Neanderthals, Sasquatch's or any of the other varieties that

were already evolving on earth on their own. No, it was

only a small number of Eris's descendants that managed to

integrate into these groups. Their numbers always low, the

reason they joined was survival. Those that have survived

are as much a part of this world as humans, their influence

on the human psyche, unquestionable.

***

The Yowie of Australia, also of Hys ancestry, is a

common creature in Aboriginal Legend, the story has

carried down in their oral history, said to stand between six

to twelve feet high. The enormous footprints often irregular

in shape and numbers of toes, if you understand the lineage

of Eris's descendants the deformed feet should come as no surprise.

The Yowie had many moods and personalities, most were timid quiet creatures. There were a few however, that showed violent aggressive behavior. They had retained a close relationship with the ocean and always returned there to die. Henry James McCooey who was an amateur naturalist wrote an account in the Australian Town and Country Journal that he called, the "Australian Apes." In the story, Henry said he saw an "Indigenous Ape while he was exploring the coast of New South Wales in an area between Batemans Bay and Ulladulla.

**

Not every sightings is a descendant of Eris as you may have noticed. I should mention a few more of these animals. There is the Yeren, who they say is living in the remote forests of Hubei, close to where the king terrorized the native people. Yeren described as a large bi-pedal ape, many suspect that it evolved from the gentle Gigantopithecus. Others argue it is a new species of Orangutan the most popular belief is that they are nothing more than figments of people's imagination.

Which may also be true of the Sasquatch like creatures reported on the Islands of Japan and in the Hibayama mountains. This creature is most likely the memory of their ancestors rising taking a path through time those only memories can travel. Like the windigo from Quebec an animal who wandered through the bush naked and had a taste for native flesh. Personally, I think there must have been some bad water in Quebec the mind can play nasty tricks on ones peace of mind.

The Nguio Rung or Batutut, some say it still lives in the area called Vu Quang in Vietnam were many new animals and fauna have recently been discovered. Many believe the Batutut is another case of a surviving species of Neanderthal or Homo erectus. Described as being close to six feet tall traveling in small groups. Occasionally seen alone, most sightings occur when the animals are foraging for fruits and leaves. Langur monkeys and flying foxes, are on the rungs menu the forest man is aggressive, human killings and mutilations have happened.

The last one we shall mention is the Chimiset or Nandi bear from Africa. The locals describe them as a cryptic creature named after the Nandi tribe. From all accounts, it looks like a bear or hyena. Some implying that if a short faced hyena that lived half a million years ago had survived it would explain the sightings. All I know is they are not Eris's descendants.

People have given us many names over the centuries, not all of them flattering. When the Kwakiutl talked about the bush people, they have seen, many said it was just someone who had gotten lost and was now a "Tsunukwa" a wild woman who went by many names. Others said no, it was "Bukwas" or "Bakwas," who was not even a creature but a spirit associated with the ocean and those that had died there. "Bakwas" also went by the names "King of Ghosts" and "Man of the Sea." However, my favorite and the one I consider the Kwakiutls most accurate description is the name, "Be'a'-nu'mbe," which means Brother of the woods.

Times have changed and not all North American Natives believe in the Sasquatch these days. When humans were closer to the land, their senses more in tune with the environment they noticed movement and sounds in ways that would make modern humans look blind and deaf.

I should not say like children, because children's senses can be in tune to the old ways. They lose these abilities as they grow. Humans of the past still had their intuition sixth sense and psychic abilities still possessed by most animals to this day. It is difficult for modern man to except the existence of a creature that most of you are no longer even able to perceive. This gives the few Sesqua still surviving, a huge advantage in being able to avoid humans.

Now that we have covered some of Eris's family tree, let us

look at another branch on that tree started by Tar that

fruitful night and some of the interactions the Nogad had

with them.

***

PROPHETS AND SHAMANS

The time after the Big Little Bang was an active period, life was flourishing on land and in the oceans. There was Eris's offspring raising hell, along with multitudes of animals that arose and spread across the land. Beavers half the size of their modern day cousins dammed the rivers, as birds of all feathers flocked the skies.

The oceans teemed with life it was an exciting yet tenuous time even for us. The Nogad concentrated on improving their propulsion systems, becoming experts in maneuvering in all fluids, while hiding in plain sight. We continued to forage on land and under the sea for the rare materials and products we needed.

The Nogad had discussed human evolution for centuries. Not ones to interfere if possible, the first response had been to let nature take its course. Many species had gone extinct and odds were humankind would follow the same path. This plan almost came to fruition seventy thousand years ago, when human numbers dropped below ten thousand. Extinction was close but the stone men survived. It was around this time the Nogad decided to take more of a hands-on approach with the human race.

***

Clouds as black as coal hug the ground, flashes of light illuminate the darkness. A streak of color dives through the clouds heading straight towards the ocean's surface. When impact seems imminent, it turns at the last millisecond skipping across the ocean waves encased in a ghostly fog.

Like children skipping rocks they are relishing in the experience, with silly grins on their faces they beam at one another. Nogad communication is silent, but the laughter vibrating through the ship and their bellies is infectious. The energy creates an audible sound that has a rich deep vibrating, sometimes-haunting tone.

Electric eels have the ability to generate eight hundred and sixty volts of electricity. Quite impressive for an earthling, yet it pales compared to the volts and amps the Nogad can generate and control. The craft an extension of their selves segmented into several sections, each section capable of holding water or different materials. This integrate honeycombed web controlled by the Nogad mind and aided by their understanding of electromagnetic propulsion, it truly is an amazing craft.

They are able to add impulses at specific points inside the craft, allowing for pinpoint control of movement. This produces an amazing array of colors, the Nogad energized by this interaction glow, shimmering and pulsating along with their ships. I should mention they could stop on a bean clam.

On this blustery morning, four of the Nogad had been running some propulsion tests and having some fun well they were at it. With the last modification, they had managed to increase the speed of their craft reaching speeds over seven kilometers a second on this day. Bringing the ship to an abrupt halt, the suddenness of the maneuver clearing the skies around them, looking down they see a startled young boy staring up at them.

That young boy was Ezekiel, and he had definitely seen them. As you can see in the description, he wrote which you can find in a popular collection of stories. The book written by forty different authors called the Bible. In the section named Ezekiel, it is online so I will not bother writing it all down for you it is easy to find. When Ezekiel recounted a story, he was quite animated.

"I looked and behold, a whirlwind came out of the north, a great cloud and a fire inside embracing itself," he said.

"And a brightness was about it, and out of the midst thereof as the colour of amber, out of the midst of the fire." Ezekiel and his kind had a funny way of talking.

The Nogad stared back down at the young boy on the banks of a river. Dressed in simple linens, Ezekiel unsure of what his eyes are witnessing stands transfixed shivering with excitement. The Nogad had realized in many ways this was their child an orphaned creature. One of their own kind was responsible for they did feel a certain responsibility.

Ezekiel's recount continues. "In the midst of the living beings there was something that looked like burning coals of fire, like torches darting back and forth among the living beings. The fire was bright and lightning was flashing from the fire." He was trying so hard to make sense of what he was seeing.

"And there came a voice from above the expanse that was over their heads. Whenever they stood still, they dropped their wings," he stared in disbelief.

"As the appearance of the rainbow in the clouds on a rainy day, so was the appearance of the surrounding radiance such was the appearance of the likeness of the glory of the lord. And when I saw it, I fell on my face and heard a voice speaking."

It is true, the Nogad when energized are truly remarkable creatures. The flashes of energy and colors transmitted when they are communicating or in motion is breath taking and a wonder to behold. It is little wonder

Ezekiel was overwhelmed by the experience. The Nogad

did communicate with Ezekiel, but he heard no audible

words that day, their thoughts became fragmented inside

his mind. The Nogad had communicated thoughts and ideas

meant to enlighten and inspire as always, the Nogad had

great hope this was not their first attempt at

communication, and it would not be their last.

Unfortunately, they had underestimated

humankind's ability to manipulate, changing the meaning

and purpose of the purest thoughts to suit their own

personal desires. This glitch in humankind confounds the

Nogad to this day and they cannot help but feel responsible

for the actions of Tar and Eris.

Tar had accelerated the human evolution at a faster

rate than was natural. Now with without supervision,

humans were beginning to dominate the planet. They were

beginning to consider earth their world, acting out and flexing their muscles with no guidance and few foes. The elders could see in this young man's eyes a need for guidance and this stirred a paternal instinct giving them hope for this young human and his kind. After that day, the Nogad spent many years going out of their way to try to influence humankind's evolutionary path. Like parents trying to guide a wayward child.

The Nogad continued in their efforts over the years, choosing a few good men and woman along the way, attempting to give them a path to follow. Let us be honest here, the Nogad just took whoever was available no great thought went into the choices. It was more like winning a lottery or losing one depending on how you looked at it. One of these men was John who wrote the "Book of Revelations." His first encounter with us is in this short excerpt from the Bible, John wrote in Revelations.

***

"After this I looked up, and behold a door was opened in heaven. And the first voice which I heard was as it were of a trumpet talking with me which said, come up hither, and I will shew you things which must be hereafter."

"And immediately I was in the spirit. And, behold, a throne was set in heaven, and one sat on the throne."

It had been an idea with good intentions we had invited him in and shown him one of the possible futures in the hope of enlightening humankind. In hindsight, one must marvel at the ability of the human memory that can slightly alter the meaning of even the purest communication. It has happened so many times throughout the Nogad many dealings with humankind that we do not really see the humor in it any more.

I mentioned before that the Nogad live their long lives inside their homes, which is true. They never leave home in the physical form, but they are able to travel outside their bodies as energy. You might call it astral traveling, it was in this state that they met a young woman in the area of Beth Fasi'el near Palmyra. Examples of the interactions between us run throughout history, although your history fails to mention the pivotal roles woman have had in your history. Her name never remembered, a story all but forgotten, if not for two inscriptions.

She was a wise young girl by all accounts and was not consumed by the individuality of men, learning the lessons with an eager respect, once again they saw hope for the human race. She called the Elders Jinnaye, a word of respect in her language. She lived in Beth Fasi'el near Palmyra, and her son inscribed the following words, "Jinnaye" and the "good and rewarding gods," in stone. This was in the days before Islam and once again, we learnt how our words and ideas could change in humankind's world as they move through time.

***

The Aboriginals of Australia have shared stories in their oral history going back to biblical times. Referred to as the "clever men" or "men of high degree" the shaman have described many encounters were they rose into the air and had meeting with the "Sky Gods." The shaman felt they had died and been brought back to life.

In the initiation ceremony of the Shaman, the chosen one is either a volunteer or some poor unsuspecting soul. Then without warning the new recruit was spontaneously attacked by the spirits, who then ritualistically slaughtered the victim. After this harrowing experience, the new shaman would have an out of body journey to a strange realm. That is where he meets the "Sky Gods."

While there the Shaman listened to the thoughts of the Nogad, who taught them about enlightenment personal empowerment and all the other wise thoughts that had been shared with humans the world over. The Shaman now a truly clever man, returned to earth to teach his people. The aboriginals of Australia called the Nogad, the "Sky Gods." In North America, the Zuni called the Nogad, the "Sky People."

Living in the area now referred to as New Mexico, the Elders of the Zuni tribe still perform ancient ceremonies that take a lifetime to understand. These secret rituals have a lot to do with the sky people.

The ceremonies performed in an ancient Zuni dialect, which only the truly dedicated can understand. The Zuni Elders have passed down their interactions with the Nogad orally, since the beginning of their consciousness. Most today would not understand the wisdom of the Zuni ancestors. Some members of the Kachina Society are trying to share the wisdom of their ancestors, however most youth of today have closed their minds at an early age.

Near by the Hopi who descended from the same Pueblo people as the Zuni, the Hopi also have many stories about the Kachina. A word the Hopi use to describe their interactions with the "Sky Warriors," or "Sky People."

It baffles the Nogad how the same actions taken in different regions of the world could have such radically different interpretations. The Kwakiutl braves in western Canada saw the experience through different eyes. The Sente and Mink legends shared below are examples of different perspectives and people's interpretations of those events.

***

A man lived in yekwin.

When asked he said, "I have come down from above. I am the son of the sun."

His name was Sente and when he first arrived, he wore the sun mask. Searching for a good place to live he found some good land by the mouth of a river. On the point, overlooking the bay there was a meadow protected from the ocean waves.

It was there that Sente built his house. When his dwelling was complete, he took off his mask and became a man for the first time. After becoming a man, Sente traveled to Bella Bella where he met a native named Brave.

Brave asked him, "How long have you been in the world as a man?"

Sente believed he had become a man recently but said, "Since the mountains were first put down." Then Sente asked Brave, "When did you become a man?"

"Behold, I have been a man for a long time" said Brave, "I became a man at the same time the kelp was first put down on the water."

That was all they said to each other, then they parted ways. Sente went home and Brave did the same. Sente apparently got itchy feet soon after and went off to explore the world.

The Mink legend one of the oldest Kwakiutl stories, so it is understandable that with time small misunderstandings filter down, getting larger. They do not detract from the essence of the story. In this tale, the mother who was to be the future mother of "Born to be the Sun" was sitting weaving wool.

***

With her back to the door, she looked towards the rear of the building as she sat on her bed weaving her wool. She felt the warmth of the sun as it caressed her back, slivers of sunlight reaching through the small cracks in the wall and ceiling. She had no husband, no man that shared her bed, yet she became pregnant and soon gave birth to a son.

He was immediately given the name "Born to be the Sun," because everyone knew his mother had become pregnant when the sun had shone on her back. Other children picked on "Born to be the Sun," because he had no father. Bluebird was the meanest, teasing the boy.

He ran to his mother's crying, "They call me an orphan, because I have no father."

His mother said, "Your father is the sun."

Immediately Born to be the Sun said, "I must go visit my father."

His mother went to her uncle who was a medicine man and made a request. "Make arrows for this child, so he may go visit his father."

The medicine man agreed and made four arrows for the boy. Born to be the Sun took the arrows, shooting them into the sky one after another in rapid succession. Each arrow hitting the shaft of the one fired before, all four arrows sticking together before falling back to earth. His mother picked up the arrows shaking them violently, she turned them into a long rope.

"Don't be foolish at this place you are going," she warned.

With that said the boy began to climb upward to visit his father, he climbed until he had climbed through to the other side of the sky. When he had climbed to the other side, he sat down in front of his father's house.

A young man saw him and asked, "Why are you here?"

"I am here to see my father said," "Born to be the Sun."

The young man went and told his elder, "This boy sitting outside, says he is here to see his father."

"Ah, ah, ah, ah, indeed, I obtained him from shining through, see if he will come in."

Boy who was to be "Born to the Sun" went and sat with his father and his father cared for him and taught him many things. His father told him that he was tired and that it was time for his son to walk in his shoes. His father cautioned him.

"Don't rush through this journey, don't look down upon others." Then he dressed his son in the finest ear ornaments and put on his sun mask, setting him down on the trail to begin his journey.

The father watched from above and warned his son again, "Don't sweep so fast when walking along, don't let others see you when peeking through."

The boy who was "Born to be the Sun" did not listen to his father, the clouds began to disappear the world began to burn because of the child's actions. His father was furious, chasing him across the world, catching the boy just before sunset, stripping him of his powers.

He said, "Is that what I told you to do? You only get one chance," with that he grabbed "Born to be the Sun" by the neck and through him through the hole back to earth.

A canoe was paddling along when they happened upon, "Born to be the Sun."

"Is this our chief, Born to be the Sun out floating about?" they wondered.

When they touched his head with a paddle, his head popped up out of the water and he puffed, "Indeed I am "Born to be the Sun," and I have been asleep on the water for a long time." He then went ashore and traveled inland.

***

It is understandable how humans have found ways to explain events you could not comprehend. Choosing to believe you had died, or believing we were gods, or you were gods. It was your way of processing the information. The Nogads are not gods and never meant for you to believe that we were. However, human perception is truly alien to us, so mistakes have occurred.

The Nogad could not foresee the power of the individuality that humans craved. The elders saw individuality as a beautiful thing; it helped to foster new ideas and technologies and was always considered, an important part of a society's growth. Nevertheless, never before had a race of conscious individuals put themselves above the needs and rights of the society as a whole.

This was a primitive instinct, usually quickly lost by most consciously evolving species. The Nogad and Sesqua had forgotten it long ago. It still lived and thrived inside some human minds. As if, there had been an evolutionary glitch, which kept rising to the surface. All for one, one for none, thankfully you are not all inflicted with this disease.

Most Nogad have given up on their hopes of enlightening the human race. However, there were a few houses of the Nogad, who found the problem to intriguing to leave alone, spending more time observing and doing occasional experiments. Hoping it was possible to breed the glitch out of humans or find a way to suppress it or remove it permanently.

Many Sesqua found themselves drawn to the humans. When you were still very aware of your environment and surroundings, we could not hide from you as we can hide from modern man. Although you could not fully understand what we were, since you had no frame of reference. Evidence of our interactions can be found throughout your history, and in many of the stories you call folklore, legend or biblical.

The last example of prophets and shamans, we shall mention has to be the Lamas of Tibet. Humans have created many organized religions that have left a bad impression on the Nogad houses. However, Tibetan Buddhism, which originated from an animist and shamanistic belief system called Bo, is closer to the wisdom the Nogad have tried to share over the years.

The Lamas of Tibet know the Sesqua well. They call us the Meh Teh and recognize the difference between a Yeti and a Sesqua. The Lamas ability to grasp concepts, few but the Nogad understand impresses our Elders. Of course, there are always misunderstanding, as seems to be the nature of cross species communication.

***

EXODUS

Human technology was growing at an accelerating rate by the 16th century. The Nogad knew it had advanced to a point where our co-existence on this planet could not go on much longer, without discovery or possible conflict. The Nogad and Sequa began arrangements for a mass exodus, returning humans to their original balance had failed.

In our attempts, we had abducted thousands over the centuries most blissfully unaware, waking up in their beds and carrying on with their lives. The Nogad

experiments have failed to find an answer. Humankind
continues to evolve now it has become the most dominant
species on the planet. Earth's atmosphere no longer held
the Nogad ships captive, most were ready to leave. We had
always considered ourselves guest on this planet. Earths
time was no longer on our side. The Nogad see time on a
different line then humans. They consider it a consequence
of movement. My elder explained it to me this way.

"In a stagnant universe there is no time, movement
creates time. Movement is what gives time the illusion of a
past, present, and future. We move through time, time does
not move through us."

The Nogad's understanding of these principles
allowed them to foresee futures not set in stone and a past
that may not happen. Movement creates change. Therefore,
no future or past can be the same. This simple concept
explained why they sucked at predicting the future,
however it was all the Nogad needed to open the door to

time travel. That is how the Nogad explain time. I hope to understand it someday.

***

On the morning of April 14th 1561, there was a great flurry of activity, the excitement building between the Nogad and Sesqua had been escalating for some time now. It was time for most of us to leave earth the Nogad had perfected the propulsion systems. Now their understanding of time had progressed beyond just the ability to glimpse into possible futures.

At sunrise, the largest of the Nogad craft rose from the oceans depths, fully charged its excitement obvious, so large it almost blocked the sun from view. As if on cue ships of various sizes emerged, some alone others in groups they buzzed about in an excited dance waiting for the last stragglers to arrive. Then with great plumes of vapor marking their exit, they left this planet and all its problems behind.

Hans Glaser wrote an article in the April 1561, issue of the Nuremberg paper. Printed on broadsheet and accompanied with a woodcut depicting the scene. I have provided a rough translation of his text below.

"In the morning of April 14, 1561, at daybreak, between 4 and 5 a.m. a dreadful apparition occurred on the sun, this was seen in Nuremberg in the city. Before the gates, and in the country, seen by many men and women. At first there appeared in the middle of the sun two blood-red semi-circular arcs, just like the moon in its last quarter, and in the sun above and below and on both sides, the color was blood, there stood "a round" ball of partly dull, partly black ferrous color."

"Likewise there stood on both sides and as a torus about the sun such blood-red ones and other balls in large number, about three in a line and four in a square, also some alone. In between these globes, there were visible a few blood-red crosses. Between which there were blood-red strips."

"Becoming thicker to the rear and in the front malleable like the rods of reed-grass, which were intermingled, among them two big rods. One on the right, the other to the left, and within the small and big rods there were three, also four and more globes."

"These all started to fight among themselves, so that the globes, which were first in the sun, flew out to the ones standing on both sides. Thereafter, the globes standing outside the sun, in the small and large rods, flew into the sun. Besides the globes flew back and forth among themselves and fought vehemently with each other for over an hour."

"When the conflict in and again out of the sun was most intense, they became fatigued to such an extent that they all, as said above, fell from the sun down upon the earth. 'As if they all burned,' and they then wasted away on the earth with immense smoke."

***

Carl Jung in 1958 wrote about the above text, "If the UFO's were living organisms, one would think of a swarm of insects rising with the sun, not to fight one another but to mate and celebrate the marriage flight."

Was he trying to debunk us? I wonder if he had any idea how close to the truth these words were. The Nogad and their craft are living organisms and that was a celebration, many were as happy to leave, as they had been to arrive. Those that left earth did not leave alone, many took humans with them.

***

ABDUCTIONS

Most people would admit they have forgotten moments. Some may even say they have lost days or weeks especially if they ever drank too much. Gaps in the human memory are common. It is something we have relied on over the years.

Abduction, the word sounds so sinister. We can understand why you would feel that way, the Nogad have abducted thousands of humans over the centuries with the help of the Sesqua. The intent had never been sinister, the tests and experiments where an attempt at trying to figure out how to fix a human abnormality we felt responsible for.

Memory masking and suppression techniques were not always one hundred percent effective. This turned out not to be that big of a deal, because of the stigma modern society puts on matters they do not understand.

***

In the 1970's on a summer evening in August, four friends on a camping trip to the backwoods of Maine had decided to do some night fishing. The two brothers, Jack and Jim Wiener collected firewood and started to build a fire that would be visible from a distance. While Chuck Rak and Charlie Foltz packed drinks and fishing gear into the canoe.

Stacking the fire high, the four set out onto the lake to catch some fish. They had only been on the water for a short while when all four of them noticed a large light in the sky. The twins and Chuck totally freaked out, starting to paddle towards shore as quickly as they could. Well Charlie

Foltz sat calmly looking back, urging his friends to stop.

The next thing any of them remembered they were sitting

on the beach, their bonfire now just a smoldering pile of

coal and ash. Hours had passed but this did not appear to

puzzle them, or seem important in any way.

Talking among themselves, they all remembered the

bright strange light. They all noticed that the fire was

almost out, but it did not seem to register. As if they did not

have a care in the world, they crawled into their sleeping

bags and fell asleep. In the morning as they were driving

down the road, they noticed a park ranger and stopped to

ask him what the strange light had been. He told them it

had been a search light, looking for a lost camper.

The boys satisfied with the explanation,

went home and would have lived normal lives if not for a

fluke accident twelve years later. When Jim Wiener fell

fifteen feet and landed on his head. The resulting injury

gave him a severe case of epilepsy and unlocked strange

visions and nightmares. Concerned, he talked to his

Doctors about the visions and they told him he was most

likely bonkers.

Not willing to except this diagnoses, he searched

out a hypnotist. Jim and Jack, along with Charlie and

Chuck participated in the study. Each man sat in a separate

room and underwent three hours of hypnosis, and they all

remembered the same experience.

They said the light had been a spaceship and that

they had been kidnapped right out of their canoe, then

taken to a large room that looked like a vet's office. The

men reported invasive tests and said they had

communicated telepathically with the aliens. It can be hard

to shut the Nogad up sometimes. When the Nogad were

finished with their experiments, they dropped them off on

the beach. If not for that knock on the head, no one would have ever heard this story.

This has worked to our advantage over the years on the odd occasions we have been accidently spotted. Most people do not believe their own eyes and quickly convince themselves that it did not happen. We like to think we have a little influence on this phenomenon, though it could be all you. The Ezekiel's and Johns of past days would not be taken seriously in this modern world, if anyone spoke of such things most would be locked up in your mental hospitals. More likely, hiding in plain view as your homeless, or maybe living in a mountain cabin. One would not have to look far to find someone with a story, they just might not be willing to share. Fear of ridicule might be the reason, or there is the possibility they really do not remember.

***

Slocan Lake B.C. the 1980s, four friends enjoying the summer had stumbled upon a natural hots springs along a lonely stretch of road. Their first day had been so enjoyable they decided to stay for another day.

The next morning Brian had gotten up with the birds, which is about an hour before the sun even gets up. Sneaking out of the tent so the other three sleepyheads could continue recharging their batteries, he walked up the hill towards the largest of the three pools.

The hot pools put together by whoever felt like doing it. They had used thick plastic bits of lumber and twine to hold the hot tubs together, letting the hot spring water trickle in. Then slowly trickled out it, was not nearly as trashy as it sounds, it had a rugged natural beauty back in its day.

The strong smell of sulfur hung in the morning air, biting at his nostrils. He found the odor refreshing on his short journey up the hill, turning the final corner Brian

stopped in his tracks! He could make out a large dark shape

soaking in the hot pool, the one that he was planning to use

for his morning dip. Not believing his eyes Brian turned

and slowly started to side step his way back down the trail,

as quietly and quickly as he could.

When he felt he was in the clear, he turned and ran

down to the tents as quickly as he could, arriving there just

as Jennifer, Allen and Bonnie were crawling out of their

sleeping bags. They see Brian running down the hill,

glancing over his shoulder every now and then.

Bonnie notices as Brian gets closer, that he has a

grin from ear to ear on his face.

"You guys are not going to believe what I just saw"

Brian says, tickled by whatever has grabbed his funny

bone. He stands there grinning at them.

"Well, spit it out then darling," Bonnie says.

"I went to take a dip in the big pool and when I came around the last corner, there was an animal sitting in there having a morning soak. It was his words trail off as he looks at their puzzled faces, deciding he would rather show them then tell them, he motions for them to follow him up the hill.

Puzzled by his excitement and now curious the four of them headed up the hill. Brian leading the way, the other three anxious to see Brains mystery animal with their own eyes. They walked up the hill as quietly as they could so as not to disturb whatever it be. When they got close to the pool, they slowed and cautiously peeked around the last bend. Sitting in the pool was a beautiful specimen, over five hundred pounds of very relaxed, black bear. Not wanting to bother him the four friends decided to go into

Nakusp, and let the bear use the hot pools for the day. They would come back to the hot pools that evening.

It was a beautiful night, they were glad they had returned. Sitting in the hot pool drinking beer and sipping on Sambuca they looked out across Slocan Lake, as the northern lights danced across the star filled sky.

They have no memory of Jenny saying, "Hey what is that?"

No memory of them all seeing the light as it got closer, or of the time they had lost, they all woke up in their sleeping bags remembering a wonderful night with friends in an amazing place and those northern light had been spectacular. Yes, it had been a night to remember. Maybe a little too much alcohol, but that seems to be a reoccurring theme through time.

***

DISSAPEARANCES

Felix vanished in 1953. A pilot for the United States
air force, he was flying over the Canadian border when he
spotted a UFO. Moncla chased the craft as ground crew
tracked them on radar. Traffic controllers witnessed both
aircraft merging on their screens and then disappearing.
Felix Moncla and his plane were never found, his abduction
a consequence of coincidence. He had joined the Nogad on
their journey because he would not back off.

Improvising is sometimes necessary. Felix became
one of thousands that left earth with the Nogad. If things
did not work out here, we wanted a future for some of you.

We are family, no matter how delinquent you are. An exodus was taking place, beginning in the sixteenth century, those that left were taking a few humans with them. We have heard suspected numbers but it was never about a specific number. We wanted to give those we took a fair chance, so we took thousands.

***

The clouds coming off the sea hugged the ground as they invaded the coastline, running up the hill. A battalion of men from the Royal Northfork regiment, their figures shrouded in the mist follow the clouds up the hill. The year is 1915 and they are on the coast of Turkey fighting in the first of the world wars in a little bay named Sulva.

From a vantage point a few hundred yard away three young men who were members of a New Zealand field company, observed the battalion. They watched as the men marched up the hill and straight into a low hanging cloud, and then disappeared into the mist.

Then they watched in amazement as the cloud lifted into the sky and vanished, blending in with the other clouds in the sky. The young New Zealanders unsure of the technologies the Turkish possessed reported to their commanders that they saw the entire battalion vanish.

Three years later the war had ended. The British government still believing their battalion had been captured and held as prisoners, demanded the Turkish government give back there men. This came as a total shock to the Turkish government, who insisted they had no knowledge of the missing battalion. The British and Turkish decide to keep this disappearance secret for over fifty years. If you are in a hurry and there are a lot of you leaving, as was the case for some Nogad in 1930, why not take a village of two thousand people.

**

Trapper Joe Labelle was on his way to visit a small community of Inuit that he knew well. The Inuit are a friendly people. Willing to give you the sealskin off their back and share their wives warmth with you if they really like you.

Joe trudged into the small community, the snowshoes on his feet giving him a bow legged silhouette. There is no one to tease him about his stance or the icicles he was wearing as a beard. He looked around perplexed. He had seen no tracks on his way here. Searching in the dwellings and storefronts produced no one, his yells met silence, not even a dog barked. The only thing he found was a small fire smoldering in one of the buildings, this told him they had only recently left.

Joe walked to the nearest town and brought the authorities back with him. They did a complete search of the area finding no tracks leaving the Inuit village. It does not snow that often in the Inuit land, this surprises many people and meant a mass exodus should have been visible. What was disturbing to the searches was the discovery of a mass grave of sled dogs under twelve feet of snow. Even more disturbing to the men was the discovery that the Inuit sacred burial ground no longer held their ancestors. The bodies had disappeared along with the Eskimos.

The Inuit had asked the Nogad if they could bring the bones of their ancestors on the journey. Since they had always been such accommodating host, the elders found it impossible not to grant their wish. Unfortunately, the bodies of their dogs could not make the journey but it does not mean they never made the journey. The Eskimos that vanished that day never returned. The next story hides in plain sight, those that share the story stretch it to unbelievable proportions, making it easy to dismiss as pure hogwash.

***

Five thousand people vanished from Stonehenge as one version goes. No, one thousand hippies disappeared. Volkswagens and everything else they owned disappeared went another account of the tale. In fact, twenty-five men, woman and children, vanished that night. They had arrived at Stonehenge with one purpose on their mind, children of the 60s generation, they had opened their minds to the possibility of life on other planets, alternate realities and beliefs. Therefore, it made sense they had come to this place they believed ancient people had used Stone Hedge to communicate with their gods, or beings from other worlds.

They set their six tents in a semi-circle. All except the children sat in the circle partaking in peyote tea and passing joints around getting themselves ready for an out of body experience. They had come with the hope of contacting aliens, had any off them believed it would actually happen? No, they were very surprised and blown away that is what one hippy kept saying, "blown away, blown away," is all he could say until he finally came down. Truthfully, I think the children find these experiences a lot easy to accept.

Witnesses described the severe thunderstorm that blew through Salisbury plain that night as intense but quick, lightning bolts struck trees and lit the area up in an eerie light. Two witnesses, a police officer and a farmer, said they saw lightning bolts strike the stones, the stones then lighting up with an intense blue light. The cop and the farmer said the light emitted from the stones was so bright that they had to cover their eyes.

It was then that they heard the screams of many people. The two men ran down to the area expecting to find dead and injured strewn about. The scene they found was not what they had expected there were no dead bodies. A complete search of the area turned up no injured hippies, not even a body part. The hippies, as the locals called them had come to Stonehenge in the hopes of contacting aliens. The Hippies, their wishes fulfilled joined the Nogad on a journey to the stars.

After 1980, there were only four families of Nogad left on earth, the houses that bore Tar and Eris and two houses with their own agendas. Everyone else has left earth and taken the few humans they could with them, my house remains because we are responsible for the mess this world is in and must find a way to save it, or die trying.

***

If you have ever owned a vehicle there is a good chance it has failed you at least once. Therefore, it should come as no surprise that over the centuries, the Nogad have encountered problems with their craft. True, it is organic technology, but even the mighty Nogad can get sick.

This next story is not about a disappearance, but the inability to disappear. A healthy Nogad has no problems hiding from curious eyes and technology. You would think with only a few Nogad left on earth the chance of every seeing one would be a dream. Normally I would agree, but the Nogad had not realized the extent of the damage humans have done to the earth and its oceans, pollution is harder on their systems than expected.

They had survived the loss of their home planet, endured the harsh voyage through space to a new land, flourishing in the new environment. Yet the greatest risk to our survival is now an animal that we helped create, rather ironic I would say.

The Nogad had been quick to adapt but the effects were noticeable. One early Christmas morning in 1994, near the coastal town of Gosford Australia, a sick Nogad was having trouble with their propulsion and guidance systems. Witnessed by hundreds of people that day the difficulties were embarrassing. It is no fun being sick, it is even worse when bunches of people are watching as you puke out your bowels.

Doctors, lawyers, academics, politicians and other respected people all came forward to say they had seen the strange craft sucking up water and then discharging large quantities back onto the lake. Many people woke up when they heard a loud noise they said had their dogs start barking and acting strangely. The large number of reports and the similarity in their nature baffled the authorities.

The local paper the Weekly Sun reported on the event and by New Years, the Weekly had received numerous calls from people who had witnessed the incident. Many reported seeing the same event. They often described beams of light emitting from the underbelly of crafts, themselves brilliantly lit. Well hovering over the water, either sucking it up or boiling it, definitely disturbing the water in some way. Nogad avoid detection at all cost, this was an embarrassing day for the Nogad. They do not like getting spotted, especially on a day when they were not at their best.

Moira McGhee, a leading UFO researcher, did an investigation into the sightings at Gosford Bay. McGhees was looking into many possibilities. Probes asked if the area was a launching site for planes or secret military craft. The Gosford Bay sightings remain a mystery to this day, the inquiries leading nowhere.

The young Nogad who got sick that day in front of hundreds knew the reason, after unwittingly ingesting large amounts of blue green algae called cyanobacteria a naturally occurring poison with potent neurotoxins. Some smart ass suggested that he had swallowed a cane toad, but this was pure silliness. The blueish green algae very seldom had large blooms but with the advances in modern agriculture, this has changed.

The toxin on the Murry River in New South Wales, Australia was half a foot thick. There was an article written in 1878 by George Francis in a magazine called, "Nature," in it he described the river this way, "A thick scum like green oil paint, some two to six inches deep." There were reports of many animals dying when they ingested the scummy water.

Cyanobacteria thrive in wastewater. The nutrient rich run off from agriculture combined with the increased use of fertilizers and pesticides the world over have turned the helpful bacteria into a menace, it is capable of producing bioactive compounds that have anticancer, antiviral and antifungal properties that are very useful to the Nogad and Sesqua.

***

THE STRANGE MAN

What Tar had started millions of years ago could not be reversed, the houses of Tar and Eris had tried in many ways to guide humans on their journey. As a member of the same Nogad house as Tar, I have always felt a certain responsibility and affection for humans and have sworn to eliminate all of Eris's and her children's spawn, that mean humans harm.

***

On a snow covered mountain in a little wood cabin covered in moss, sits a strange man, he has not drank alcohol in many years, tonight he drinks not to forget but to try to remember. The firelight was flickering in and out of the creases on his nose. This being the only prominent feature on his face besides the silver beard that rose above his cheekbones and joined his eyebrows in a twisted pact. He looks around the room nervously as if expecting something to happen.

Beside the door sits a 30/30 Winchester cocked and loaded, two sticks of dynamite hang from his belt as he settles into the chair and rocks back and forth, back and forth pausing occasionally to listen intently. Hearing only the snaps from the fire and the soft thud of the snow he sniffs the air and then sniffs again, his nose wrinkled as he tries to recognize the scent he has picked up.

The old bloodhound silent by his feet lets out a sigh as she rocks to her feet and slinks across the room, spinning in a tight circle three times before lying down beside the woodstove with a deep sigh, she feels nervous around drunk people. The strange man sniffs the air again before letting out a raucous laugh.

"Dang dog, what you been eating? Bad enough to gag a skunk," he bellows as he washes down the smell with a mouthful of Jack Daniels Black.

Talking to no one and the dog at the same time, he starts to remember. The hound's eyes shut and she is soon pretending to be asleep. The man's eyes grow large as he remembers a sliver of an event that hangs behind a dark fog in his memory banks, like a dream, no a nightmare one he feels he should remember but never can.

Fueled by a twenty-six of Jack, with his audience of one snuggled asleep by the fire, he forgets his vigil at the door taking another large swig, determined to remember, he begins to recount the events aloud.

"I was up above the tree line, only a few hours of good daylight left. With a lot of miles to cover three thousand feet of elevation to lose, I was in a hurry, and I'd left Sally," the dogs ears perk up for a second at the sound of her name, then relax, "behind for the day, as she was getting to old to keep up," he reaches down and scratches behind the hound's ear, absent mindedly.

The alcohol is slowly lifting the fog, the memories begin to reveal themselves. He pauses taking another swig and adjusts the sling he has on his right arm before going on with the story he is hearing for the first time.

"Cutting across a slide area my foot dislodged a large boulder that went flying down the chute path, I yelled at the top of my lungs "ROCK COMING DOWN," to warn anyone who might be below."

He looks around the room nervously as if afraid someone other than the hound had felt the vibrations of his words, he was not supposed to remember but he has remembered. In silence, he remembers the rock picking up speed as it careened its way down the hill, the silence that followed his warning screams.

No one answered his call an hour later he still found himself cutting back and forth across the mountain losing elevation at a steady rate and using the slide shoot as a boundary on his way down, then he heard a sound. Remembering that sounds brings the story back to his dry lips, he moistens them with another shot and continues his memory no longer blocked.

"That sound froze my heart, I don't usually get scared or fear anything in the bush but this had an unnatural feel, something was coming up the slide chute straight up the shoot at a very quick speed." He had stopped and backed himself into a large cedar tree, as if he was trying to merge with it, he watched as the creature came up the hill.

The strange man recalls, "It seems to read the ground at a glance, running on his toes every step landing calculated to leave the smallest imprint."

Surprisingly fast for his size. he comes to a stop and rises on two feet to look around.

"He knew I was near, he stayed on two legs as he headed up the steep embankment towards me using his hands only for balance."

Again, the cabin falls silent as the memory retreats to its silent narrative inside his mind, the memory of what he saw as he tried to melt into the mountainside still playing tricks with his mind.

The strange man had not been in my sites that day, I had been on the trail of one particularly nasty killer tracking him into the high country. To get ahead of my prey I had traveled miles to the south staying on the downwind side in the next valley, aware any unintentional sounds would hit the ridge bouncing over any listening ears. Hey it happens, no matter how sure your feet are in certain areas especially slides chutes it is possible to knock rocks loss. Circling quickly, I gained the higher ground on my prey. Waiting in silence as he climbed the hill, 1000 yards below me and closing fast, I prepared for my attack, suddenly the beast stopped.

Had he spotted me? The wind was not in his favor he would not have smelt me then I saw the human, tucked into the crotch of a cedar tree sat a little man frozen in fear, why had I not noticed this little man is strange?

The alcohol releases the last of the buried memory and the strange man continues his story.

"It charged straight towards me, traversing the rocky terrain on the surest of legs, rage in its eyes, it closes the distance between us in seconds. I knew I was going to die a horrible death, suddenly out of nowhere appeared a larger beast that grabbed the other by the neck and threw him down the hill, leaving me staring in disbelief."

Had it really happened, the bottle slips from his fingers and lands on the floor teetering for a second before settling, standing straight up not a drop spilt. The dog looks up as if expecting to hear more of the story, snorting once before settling into her own slumber once again.

My battle with the beast did not last long, I take no pleasure in killing but some creatures should not walk this earth, grabbing him by the throat I had snapped his neck and tossed him down the hill, following after him disappearing from the man's sight in seconds. If the strange man ever chose to share his story, he would have a tall tale to tell.

The strange man snores a sorrowful tune crumpled in a fetus position he sleeps were he fell, a bottle half full in his outstretched hand. The strange man awakens with a start, with bloodshot eyes he tries to focus, his eyes come to rest on the familiar shape of the bottle. Dishes piled high in the sink, no idea how long he has been sitting there trapped in a whirlpool of jack black and memories he could not fully grasp as they swirled by his whiskey soaked mind. Sleeping on the floor where he fell of his chair, he staggers to his feet and bounces off the doorframe, on his way for a morning piss. Air, frozen and crisp burns his nostrils as he exits the cabin, scanning the visible terrain he stumbles, fumbling to unzip his wool pants a groan of relief escapes his lips and a crude rendition of his name is scribbled half dribbled into the snow.

Entering the cabin he falls on both knees in front of the airtight, stoking the fire with one hand as the other strokes his disheveled beard. The question he feels have been answered, he takes one last swig from the bottle in his hand and ponders the truth he now knows. Feeling eyes on him he looks over to his right and notices a familiar friend.

"So you mangy mutt, what do you think?"

He pauses as if expecting an answer, gently massaging the dog's head the strange man throws dried kibble in the dog's bowl and puts her outside. He needs time to forget, yeah that is all he needs and he chuckles to himself as his head tilts back and the warm liquid slides down his throat once more.

This time he drinks to forget, not to remember. Not everyone can handle the truth, the Strange man knew that much. Don't worry about the strange man, he put that bottle down and made peace with himself. Deciding that it had all been a bad dream, it was not a story he chose to share, let

alone try to exploit.

HOAXES AND RUMORS

People call it the Devils Triangle. Many planes and ships have disappeared in this area, the supposed location of many abductions. The stories have gained popularity over the years. The most famous, being the disappearance of flight 19 in 1945. When five United States Navy TBM Avenger torpedo bombers went missing along with the fourteen aviators.

The story made famous in the Steven Spielberg movie, "Close Encounters of the Third Kind." Incredibly, on that same day, the PMB Mariner BuNo 59225 went missing with thirteen on board well it was searching for flight 19.

In 1947, a B-29 was lost that is the story. On the other hand, there is no record of a B-29 ever being lost in that area. Nevertheless, many people still believe it happened and the legend grows. Many people and planes disappeared over the years, there were also reports of ships going missing, and the documentation on them goes back to the early 1800s.

Ninety souls lost on the USS Pickering.

One hundred and forty lost on the USS Wasp.

Three hundred and sixty lost on the USS Cyclops.

The tragedies go on I wish we could say we took those people. The events do lead one to the conclusion that it is some kind of abduction area. Sadly, natural events caused those disappearances not us. We would never be so obvious, especially considering your advances in technology. Although primitive, you were beginning to hamper our movements.

No matter what you have heard, we had nothing to do with flight 19 or anything else that happened at the Bermuda Triangle. Many theories abound not least of which blames aliens. Well I am here to set the record straight, we have never abducted people from the Bermuda Triangle. Not to say we have not abducted people. However, most stories are false this has aided us in our efforts to stay hidden.

Hoaxes and rumours have been around almost as long as we have. Even the cave dwellers would pull pranks on one another. Fake U.F.O. sightings have made it much easier for the Nogad's and Sesqua to remain hidden. If we were spotted these days, most people will not believe their own eyes or find explanations that made sense of the sightings. Human ability to manipulate film and photography has added to your doubt, we loved this phenomenon. The ability to spin a good tale was humankind's main form of entertainment for centuries and you have used it well.

***

A famous and long running hoax happened on the outskirts of Kansas City in the 1800s. A man named Alexander Hamilton who was a well-respected member of the community reported a most unusual occurrence that he saw one morning. He said he had walked out of the house with his son and a tenant. The three men saw an unidentified flying object hovering over his farm. Alex said it had a cigar shape and inside the craft were six humanoid forms that were trying to winch a small calf up into the airship.

On closer examination he had realized the red cable that had wrapped around the calf, was also tangled in his fence line. He attempted in vain to free the calf when he was unable to do this he cut a section of the fence free.

Then he and his companions watched in amazement as the calf and the ship rose slowly and sailed off.

This story first appeared in the Yates Center Farmers advocate, a local newspaper. Many prominent citizens of the area stepped forward to vouch for Alexander's honesty and character. The story became famous and for nearly one hundred years, many considered it one of the best examples of a U.F.O. ever documented.

The truth finally came out many years later that Hamilton along with many of the prominent citizens of the area had belonged to a local liars club. The members regularly tried to outdo each other with tall tales. The patrons had been so enthralled with the Hamilton's tall tale they had submitted it to the local newspaper as a farce, having no idea how wide the tall tale would spread. FATE magazine wrote an article eighty years later revealing the truth about the event.

***

Lights in the sky are one of the illusions used by pranksters and hoaxers the world over. Several people reported sightings of intricate lights flying in patterns and suddenly disappearing in Kent, New York. Known as the Hudson Valley sightings, a group of amateur small plane pilots called the Stormville Flyers were responsible for most of the sightings.

They would string multi colored lights onto their small planes then well flying in precise formation, the optical illusions would create spectacular patterns. Easily mistaken as spacecraft, the pilots in radio contact could with a synchronized flick of a switch, disappear from the night sky, fooling many people.

***

Another example of the silliness that helps our cause occurred on July 14th 2005. The chief executive officer of the organization searching for Bigfoot, Tom

Biscardi went on a coast-to-coast radio show called, A.M. Paranormal.

Then announced he was certain his organization would capture a Bigfoot in the near future. He said they were getting close on their hunt for the Sasquatch, in the Happy Camp area of California.

One week later, he was back on A.M. Paranormal to announce the capture of a Sasquatch and his intent to sell tickets to a pay per view event. He cancelled the event soon after, blaming a gullible public and a woman he never named for misleading him. Three years later Tom Biscardi was back in the news.

July 2008 two young men, Rick Dyer and Mathew Whitten posted a video on You Tube. Claiming they had found the dead body of a Sasquatch in the woods of Northern Georgia and now, they had it frozen inside of a freezer.

So who did they call to investigate this claim? Why, Tom Biscardi of course, the chief executive officer of Search for Bigfoot Inc. They offered Rick and William fifty thousand dollars as a good faith gesture. It was a huge media event and many of the big news networks covered the story, CNN, BBC, ABC and Fox attended.

The alleged Bigfoot arrived, frozen in a block of ice inside a freezer. An anxious crowd waited with great anticipation as the ice slowly melted uncovering two rubber feet, a hollowed out skull of unknown origins and some fake hair.

Obviously, a hoax our feet are not made of rubber. Besides we would never die on land, it is not our way. Even Eris's offspring do not leave remains the methods they use to dispose of their kin we do not approve of but they are effective.

If the last story sounded familiar, it is because it was not even original. Years before Rick and Mathew posted their video on YouTube; there was the "Minnesota Iceman."

A carnival carrying a most unusual exhibit traveled throughout the northwest of the United States. Beginning in the 60s and ending in the 70s a frozen Sasquatch was on display. Customers could view the specimen through a block of ice and it gained much attention. Two cryptozoologists heard about the find and after careful examination, they became convinced that it was real.

Ivan Sandman and Bernard Heuvelman were two cryptozoologists with a dream. This was what they had worked all their lives for and now they had an actual Bigfoot to show the world. They beat the drums and invited scientist to examine the creature. Sanderson was persistent and finally managed to get the Smithsonian to show a tiny bit of interest in buying it. However, the Smithsonian quickly changed their mind.

Just the fact that the Smithsonian had shown some interest sparked the curiosity of other scientist who wished to examine the iceman. As interest grew more intense, Frank became more evasive. Eventually he announced the "iceman" had degraded over the years and was no longer available for show. The specimen in the ice he explained was a replica, and you would think that was the end of that story.

The original story had the iceman was found encased in a three-ton block of ice, either by a Russian sealer or Japanese whaler well floating in the Siberian Sea. Eventually, it ended up in a Hong Kong deep-freeze, from there it made its way to America. Were a California millionaire bought it, for some reason he had decided to remain anonymous.

Rumours swirled and most people had no doubt that Jimmy Stewart had bought the "Minnesota Iceman." People also believed Jimmy had sent Frank Hanson on tour with the Sasquatch because he was fascinated in their reactions when they saw the creature.

Since then the story has taken another turn, Frank now says he was out hunting and shot the creature himself. Truly, a talented storyteller and showman thank you for your stories Frank. People like you have helped keep us safe. Franks nature would not allow him to see let alone shoot one of us, no offence Frank, just the way it is.

***

What visions come to mind when you hear the name Bigfoot, do you imagine a huge hairy beast with large feet or do you wonder where the name originated. It sounds like an old term first used, centuries ago. In fact, it has not been around that long, the first time the media used the term was in 1958.

When a young man working at a construction site noticed some large footprints, he got down from his tractor.

Jerry Crew measured what he realized were massive tracks over sixteen inches long. The California papers picked up the story and started calling the mythical beast that made the prints Bigfoot. The tag became popular and some say replaced Sasquatch as the popular name. I do not think you will find many Sesqua that agree with that statement.

Jerry was an extremely gullible young man. His excitement over the find was infectious. The locals knew that the young man's boss could be quite the prankster, or in this case quite a "plankster." Ray Wallace had strapped large wooden planks onto his feet and had ran around in the mud, creating new trails for young Jerry to follow, then he would sit back at a distance and take great pleasure in the young boys excited bewilderment.

Ray Wallace died in 2002. His family came clean and told everyone it was just a playful prank. To this day, there are still those that believe those footprints were real. Not all sighting of Sasquatch are fake neither are all the

UFO sightings. By now, those that believe will believe and those that wish not to believe will hold firm.

***

Recently photographs appeared on Facebook, twitter and other social media sites around the world, claiming that multitudes of witnesses from Brazil, China, and India along with other countries reportedly saw a "UFO mothership." It appeared, "semi-cloaked," in a number of heavily populated regions.

There were photos accompanying the post showing what appeared to be a large "clam" like object hovering over houses and people. The photos showed a craft partially hidden by some low flying clouds hovering over people, and buildings.

People swore the pictures were real, others mentioned that there were now phone apps that could take such photos. Long heated debates that led nowhere developed. Newspapers, tabloids is a better term, reported that the photographs were authentic. People telling the story added their own facts and the story grew getting bigger every time. I bet you could fill twenty football stadiums with people that still believe those pictures.

***

LIFE CYCLE OF THE NOGAD & SEQUA

If you made it this far, you are ready to hear about ocular and tactile evolution. For those interested, I have also written a brief explanation of the lifecycle of the Sesqua and Nogad.

The harsh and deteriorating conditions of our home planet allowed only a few, extremely hardy life forms to evolve and flourish. With oceans, barely a mile deep and disappearing quickly our ancestors had sensed the need to evolve rapidly. Moreover, they had found ways to make this happen.

Absorbing information on a cellular level they took advantage of a process we call tactile evolution. A simple explanation of the tactile process is to imagine a primitive creature, with only the most basic of functions, limited in movement an obstacle blocks its path. Primitive touch receptors receive the information absorbing and then influencing subtle changes in the next generation's genetic code.

Hunger the driving force, movement the solution in the constant search for energy. Following generations, slowly started evolving new solutions a few growing small movable fringes around the border of their bodies. Allowing water currents to flow around and beneath, the first of our ancestors lifted off the ocean floor. They had learnt a simple form of movement every time information was absorbed the process repeated itself. Small improvements in the needed direction were the result all this occurring without conscious thought. Tactile evolution was the predecessor to ocular evolution.

Ocular, is a process that uses visual information along with conscious thought to influence genetic code. To understand ocular, one would need to comprehend the electrochemical exchange between the eye and the brain. Then one might understand its ability to influence evolutionary mutations. Personally, I do not understand how this works but I know it does.

Tactile and ocular evolution turned out to be exceptionally beneficial in speeding up and shaping our evolutionary path. It does not mean changes happened over night it still took eons to accomplish our goals.

Originally, two Nogad would pair up and swim together into the ocean depths there they mated and produced offspring that would grow up in their elders protection. Eventually they learn to assist in the construction and maintenance of their houses sometimes a young Sesqua would move out and begin a new house. These were the building blocks of our society.

The Nogad realized early in their evolution that they were limited in certain abilities. They envisioned a free-swimming child and with the help of ocular evolution, the first Sesqua was born. The succeeding generations of Sesqua evolving into the varieties which exist today.

Lifespans were short in the beginning this allowed for rapid changes. It was only after reaching earth that our lifespans increased to the present ranges. The Nogad's still novices in flight out of the water spent the last few centuries on our planet evolving and mastering flight in all environments.

During this time, the Sesqua lead the way on other adventures. Leaving our protective ocean home and venturing onto land for short periods. The ability to survive on land and in the water developed more once we reached

earth, it was only then that the Sesqua became the only

truly amphibious animal in the universe, as far as we know.

The Nogad, always thinking and always aware,

have carefully controlled our population. Never wanting to

overuse the resources of earth plus a natural desire, we all

have for balance. When the Nogad are ready to increase

their population two separate houses of the Nogad will join

forces.

Sinking into the ocean depths, the mating ritual

only witnessed by Nogad eyes, now produces one male and

one female Sesqua. Spawned from the two Nogad houses,

these offspring, born at the same time are not brother and

sister, they would grow up and eventually mate, the bond

lasting for life.

The young fragile free-swimming newborns have an

average lifespan of thousands of years. For such a powerful

creature, they are born weak and vulnerable needing the Nogads constant attention and care. Attentive parents, the Nogad nurture and protect their young as they slowly grow and begin to explore the world outside gathering materials and helping the Nogad in any way possible.

After many years, the two young Sesqua begin to spend longer time away from their respective Nogad homes. Exploring the world and gathering materials together not reaching maturity until they are one thousand years of age.

The Sesqua, are caring parents and raise their young for the first five hundred years. Then watch over them through life with the help of the Nogad. Unlike their parents who are first born the children of the Sesqua are brother and sister and must find a Sesqua mate from an unrelated house. Once mated this bond also lasts for life.

Losing one's mate is a painful journey that we must

navigate through with as much grace and courage that we can muster. Lessons learnt from all experiences no matter how painful are beneficial. My Amia is no longer with us, the memory of her passing still an open wound perhaps one day I will share our story but not today.

The children of the Sesqua continue to visit the Nogad regularly during this enlightenment stage, mating and raising Sesqua when we need them keeping the population stable otherwise. Exploring the land and sea, the time spent learning and wandering is a fun time for the Sesqua their days and nights filled with adventure.

The lesson learnt and the teachings of the Nogad expanding their minds preparing them for the final cycle of a Sesqua. They seldom contemplated this fact, relishing the experiences as they lived life in the moment for thousands of years. We are then known as, Sesqua of the 10th house or a "very wise Sesqua." The Sesqua have then acquired the wisdom needed to join the Nogad. They return to their elder's home for their final visit.

A Sesqua of the 10th having accumulated the years of knowledge and experience needed for enlightenment enter the house of his or her Nogad for their final visit. To complete the transmutation a physical bond between the Nogad and the Sesqua takes place. Then the metamorphosis from Sesqua to a young Nogad begins.

Since this is a special occasion marked once every ten thousand years give or take a few thousand. The Sesqua brings a special offering to his elder handpicked from only the finest varieties, a small assortment of clams are presented to the Nogad, who take great pleasure in receiving this gift, they love clams. One could only hope to be as happy as the clams the Nogad cared for. Clams in the wild can live for over five hundred years as guests of the Nogad clams live for over one thousand years.

The homes of the Nogad are incredible structures. In fact, they are the exoskeletons of the Nogad. A young

Nogad fragile and vulnerable in its first year eagerly takes the materials we have gathered for them and absorb large amounts. Then the baby Nogad begins to secrete the material they use to expand their homes. Eating and building slowly layer by layer, they create the intricate interiors that will become their home for generations.

As mentioned, they strictly control the number of new homes built. Few Nogad build their own homes instead, they expand the homes of elder Nogad. Everyone enjoys the arrangement it saves the young Nogad years of work and the elder Nogads enjoy the company, along with the opportunity to exchange new ideas and thought.

There is an amazing animal living on earth, few people know about. Water bears, share so many of the same capabilities and traits of the Nogad. No relation, but you might think they were the way the Nogad carry on about them. Both have bodies with the structure of a liquid yet they are solid water bears were already on earth when we arrived.

Tardigrades as you call them are cute eight legged animals. Never reaching a length over half a millimetre, they can survive almost anything. Living in environments on earth ranging from the highest mountain tops to the deepest oceans. Able to withstand extreme temperatures they thrive in tropical rain forests like the amazon and frozen landscapes including Antarctic.

The incredible little Tardigrades can survive the cold irradiated vacuum of space. They do this by covering themselves in a glassy molecule impervious to even the killer radiation of space that would imbed itself in the body of almost any other living animal. Ripping apart their molecules, and damaging their DNA down to its core. That does not happen to the water bears, although perhaps one of their most amazing talents is their ability to create their

own genome.

By combining the DNA, they steal from an

assortment of bacteria, plants, and some single celled

organisms. They can acquire up to a fifth of their genome

from foreign sources, for such a simple creature, they hold

so much potential. Yes, the Tardigrades and Nogad, share

many similarities.

***

It is amazing how memory of events change over

time. In todays, modern age you have twenty-four hour

news service, video cameras everywhere. No one even

needs to rely on their memory to check facts. Yet a man

named Donald Trump can tell a story about hundreds of

Muslims celebrating in the streets of America. In addition,

even his opponent seems to remember these things

happening however; nowhere in all your miles of tapes and

recordings can you find evidence that what Donald said is true.

One man creates a reality and many follow therefore, it should be obvious how facts can twist over time. Donald is the perfect example of how this anomaly works. He reminds the Nogad of many influential people in your history who have arose to rule countries and cults. He is a man that cannot see past his own arrogance. If the American people let Donald Trump become President, I personally will be leaving this planet, until then I hold onto a little hope.

Humans have invented a system were the elite use the people below them. There is no equality. Paths are taken for the wrong reasons humans seem to only respect others if they have money, it is not necessary for them possess any redeemable characteristics or qualities.

Many live unhappy lives, trying to fill the void with escapism in any form. Well the corporations pollute your planet and put your very existence at risk. We are all on the same journey. Our goal is and always will be survival. The only way humans will fail and go extinct right now is if you let the interest of corporate greed and organized religion lead the way.

The Nogad and Sesqua have no use for material goods. Passion choses the path we follow, respect we earn with knowledge it is not bought with money. Life is an adventure of discovery and joy. We are not someone's tool. None goes without food or shelter, passion is encouraged. Those that mentor, respect new ideas and thoughts often learning from those they are teaching. We are not gods and never told you we were you came up with that on your own.

The problem is we let you, which was our mistake, now you have elevated yourselves to god like status on this little planet but shirk at your responsibilities. Your world leader's huff, puff, and dance around each other trying to empress themselves and their followers with their toughness. Like children in a schoolyard, except these children are deciding the fate of the world.

Nogad technologies have advanced beyond our wildest thoughts. Sometime one does not understand what is possible until there looked at from a different perspective. Then all of a sudden new ideas are born doors open, and we step through into new realities. One must never close their mind to new ideas. It worries us that humans have narrowed their perspective closing the door to many possibilities.

Humankind has a chance to create a beautiful world or destroy it. Some of you believe there is a God that will save you, what if no one is coming to save you. Will you watch as humankind extinguishes itself? I should apologize for my rant sometimes it is just so frustrating.

The Nogad recognize humanity's love of individuality and fear of the unknown. If you want to understand what happens when you pass over, you will have to ask the Nogad. What I have grasped is that once you have reached the enlightenment stage your energy will become part of the whole, individualism and self-awareness will be lost. According to the Elders, the loss of individuality in the realm of enlightenment is not a bad thing the energy that is not ready for this transformation remains on earth.

By the end of the 20th century, as you know most of us had left earth. The few remaining Sesqua and Nogad that have stayed on earth considerer it their home, and after fourteen million years of habitation, wish to remain. Some consider humans to be family and hope to guide them in the right direction. Others have eviler intentions. I shall remain until the end, Trump or no Trump.

Reference material in the back, if you wish to find some of the legends I have mentioned. Remember, we are all in this together no one is coming to save this world. It is up to us to find a solution and be the saviors. Should not be a problem if we all make a real effort. Preachy ending, but if an alien cannot preach who can. Have a happy life. Take care of your world. Galaglaw out.

***

ACKNOWLEGMENTS:

Male'd   (1800's)   Kwakiutl Chief

Ezekiel (622 B.C. – 570 B.C.)   (1400 BC) – "Ezekiel"

John (96 B.C. – 98 A.D.)   (0 -1 A.D.) –

"Revelations"

Strange Man (1959-1999)   a possible prophet

(unknown)

Frank Boas (1858-1942)   Kwakiutl Tales (1910)

Allagash White Water Abduction   YouTube

Wikipedia

*****

Made in the USA
Charleston, SC
22 November 2016